SO-ART-202

There's a mysterious light on *inside* the church tower! I wonder what it could be?

It hasn't gone away yet. *Finally* something exciting and mysterious is happening around here. Maybe I should investigate it—like a real detective or something. But I sort of wish the light would just go out. It's making me too curious. And I get wiggly when I get too curious.

Elspeth Campbell Murphy

BECKY GARCIA

Illustrated by Tony Kenyon

Chariot Books
DAVID C. COOK PUBLISHING CO.

A Wise Owl Book
Published by Chariot Books, an imprint of David C. Cook Publishing Co.
David C. Cook Publishing Co., Elgin, Illinois 60120
David C. Cook Publishing Co., Weston, Ontario

BECKY GARCIA
© 1986 by Elspeth Campbell Murphy

All rights reserved. Except for brief excerpts for review purposes, no part of this book
may be reproduced or used in any form without written permission from the
publisher.

Illustrated by Tony Kenyon
Cover and book design by Catherine Hesz Colten

First Printing, 1986
Printed in the United States of America
90 89 88 87 86   1 2 3 4 5

Library of Congress Cataloging-in-Publication Data

Murphy, Elspeth Campbell.
  Becky Garcia.

  (The Kids from Apple Street Church; 5)
  "A Wise owl book."
  Summary: Becky records in her journal pursuit of two mysteries: one involving
music hidden in church and another involving her brother.
  [1. Christian life—Fiction. 2. Mystery and detective stories. 3. Diaries] I. Kenyon,
Tony, ill. II. Title. III. Series.
PZ7.M95316Be 1986   [Fic]   86-8877
ISBN 1-55513-029-1

To my teacher, Mr. Kirkwood,
who encouraged me to write.

Glory to God in the Highest

December 19

Friday

Dear God,

We got out of school early today, because THIS IS THE START OF CHRISTMAS VACATION!! I have to do my afternoon dog-walking job in a little while, but now is a good time to work on my prayer journal, I think.

It is pretty quiet here in the apartment. My mother is still at the department store where she works, and my brother, Bobby, is out somewhere with his crazy friends.

I like writing to you, God. I'm glad my Sunday school teacher, Miss Jenkins, gave us notebooks so we could write prayer journals.

Bobby said I could use his new pen. He is in the grade above me, and his regular schoolteacher gave pens to Bobby's class for Christmas. Each kid got one with his own name printed right on it. So this pen says ROBERTO GARCIA, JR.

Mrs. Whitney, my regular schoolteacher, gave us pencils and candy canes.

Back on the first day of December, Mrs. Whitney let us make Christmas countdown chains. Each day you tear off a link, until you get to the last link—and then it is CHRISTMAS!! We took our chains home after the party today, so tonight I will tear off another link before I go to bed.

I am really looking forward to Christmas, God. And I am really looking forward to Christmas Eve, too. Know why? Because our church is having a Church Family Christmas Eve Party that night. And after the party, we will all go into the sanctuary and sing Christmas carols and light candles.

My family didn't go to the party last year, because we didn't live here then. Last Christmas my father was still alive. But then he was killed in a car crash last March. So now there is just my mother, my brother, and me. It makes me very sad to write about that, God.

● ● ●

Well, I think I will go now, God, and read the new mystery book I got from the library. I like to read all kinds of books, but mysteries are my most favorite.

Nothing exciting or mysterious ever happens around here. The only time anything like that happened was when someone at school took Julie Chang's doll (really it was her sister Carolyn's).

But I was absent that day, because I had to go to the dentist. So I missed the whole thing.

The book I am reading now is about these kids who are taking their summer vacation in a haunted castle. We never get to go on vacations like that.

LATER
Dear God,

Hi! I'm back from reading my book. I have to get ready for my dog-walking job, but I thought I would write some more first.

When we moved here last summer, I didn't think I would like living in an apartment building instead of our house, but it turned out to be Better Than OK.

There are two bedrooms in our apartment. My mother has one, and Bobby has the other one, because he's the older kid. So maybe you're wondering where I sleep, God. But you already know, right? Miss Jenkins, my Sunday school teacher, says you are always with us. So if you are always with me, you must always know where I am.

You know that my bedroom is in the part of our apartment that is supposed to be the dining room. But we don't use the dining room for eating, because we just eat in the kitchen.

So my mother put up a couple of folding screens and made a cozy, little bedroom where there didn't even used to be one. She put my bed and my dresser and my desk and my bookcase in there. And the furniture helps to make part of the walls.

Best of all, she fixed my room so the balcony could be part of it. Looking out of the balcony window is one of my favorite things to do.

In the summer I could open the balcony doors, and it was like sleeping in the tree-tops, because we're at the top of the building on the third floor.

My friends Mary Jo and Julie both like my different kind of room. Mary Jo especially likes the balcony. She keeps wanting to try to jump from the balcony to our tree. The tree is near the balcony, but it's not *that* near!

My mother just about has heart failure every time Mary Jo comes over, because she's afraid Mary Jo will really try to jump off the balcony one of these days. But I don't think Mary Jo would *really* do that. Would she, God?

12

Of course, there are no leaves on the tree now, because it's winter.

And that means I can see pretty far through the branches.

For one thing, I can look out and see the angels.

They aren't real angels, of course. They are just Christmas decorations on the tower of Apple Street Church across the road.

But I like to imagine they are real and

that you sent them to watch over me, God. I haven't told anyone else that—just you.

I wish my father could see the Apple Street angels. I think he would like them. But I guess it's all right, since he can see real ones.

Apple Street Church has shepherd decorations, too. The shepherds are down below on the ground with their sheep.

At nighttime there is a little light that shines on the shepherds and sheep so people can see them.

And there is a floodlight attached to a stake in the ground. It shines up on the angels on the tower. That's to make it look like the bright light the shepherds saw when the angels came to tell them about Jesus.

One of the angels is playing cymbals. One of them is blowing a trumpet. And the one in the middle is holding a banner that says, *Glory to God in the Highest*. That's what the angels said to the shepherds when Jesus was born. But, of course, you already know that, God, since you're the one who sent the angels in the first place.

Pastor Bennett says the angel decorations have belonged to Apple Street Church for about a hundred years, which is how old the church building is. Pastor Bennett talks a lot about the church building and the people who went to church there a long time ago.

I like books about people who lived a long time ago, too. But mysteries are still my favorite.

LATER

Dear God,

I hope it is all right for people to write in their prayer journals when they are mad. Because I am *so mad* at Bobby!!

I am back from dog walking now, but I would like to tell you about what happened when I was out, OK?

So I will just start at the beginning.

First of all, I went to pick up Fifi Randolph. I always get her first because it takes so long to get her ready for a walk. That's because I have to put her little hat and coat and boots on her. Fifi is the kind of dog who has painted toenails and bows on her ears. I don't know how she feels about that, but she is a poodle, so bows look OK on her.

And sometimes it's hard to get started on the walk, because old Mrs. Randolph,

16

Fifi's owner, has to complain to me about Bobby and his wild friends running all over her yard and making noise. Sometimes she even calls up my mother to complain about Bobby.

But anyway. After I got Fifi, I went to pick up Patches Johnson. Patches is not one special breed of dog—he is a mixture. I think he is mostly beagle. And as you can tell from his name, he has different colors in his fur. The colors are black and white and tan. He has a very nice personality, too.

Mrs. Johnson says that Patches really likes me and that I have a knack for making dogs do what I tell them. It was very nice of her to say that.

Our apartment building allows pets, which is lucky for me if I ever get a dog of my own. I hope, I hope, I hope.

I started the walk by going over to the church so I could look at the Christmas decorations close up. (The bad part of the walk didn't happen yet.)

I like the stable with Mary, Joseph, and baby Jesus. It's at the front of the church.

And then around at the side of the church there are the shepherds and angels.

My friend Mary Jo Bennett, Pastor Bennett's daughter, came running out when she saw me doing my dog-walking job. She brought her own dog, Bruno, with her.

Bruno is a very nice dog, but he is kind of wild and crazy. He upsets Fifi, who is kind of nervous anyway.

So we decided I would take Bruno, since he behaves almost OK for me, and Mary Jo would take Fifi and Patches, who get along pretty well together.

18

So everything worked out fine.

That is, it *would* have been fine if my BROTHER and his DUMB FRIENDS hadn't shown up.

They jumped out at us from nowhere and started throwing snowballs.

I hate snowballs. And I doubly hate it when people jump out at me.

The boys started calling, "Hey, Becky-Wecky! Hey, Jerry-Mo!"

We couldn't throw snowballs back at them because we had to hold onto the dogs.

"Quit it!" Mary Jo and I said, real loud and serious.

"Who's gonna make us? You and your big, brave poodle?"

Well, that just shows those boys don't know Fifi Randolph very well, God! Fifi is usually a very nice dog, even though she is nervous. But just don't get her mad,

20

because then there's no telling *what* she'll do!

Patches and Bruno weren't a big problem. They just wanted to play with the boys. But Fifi bared her teeth and made these deep, rumbling growls in her throat.

"Becky!" Mary Jo said. "What's the matter with Fifi?"

"Here, give me her leash," I said.

Fifi was too mad for me to pick her up, but at least I could hold on to her.

"Bobby!" I yelled. "If you don't get out of here, I'm telling!"

I felt like crying, but I didn't want him to see that.

"Oooo, Bobby!" said one of his stupid friends. "Is your little baby sister gonna tell your mommy on you?"

But Bobby knew he would be in BIG trouble with Mom if she heard about him doing one more dumb thing while she was away at work.

It was getting harder and harder to hold Fifi.

"Nice doggy," said one boy, Jeff, coming closer.

"Don't tease her!" Mary Jo warned, sounding pretty nervous herself.

"Tremble, tremble," Jeff said and laughed.

Then Bobby said, "Hey, Jeff. You'd better *start* trembling, man, if Becky lets Fifi loose."

"*Fifi!*" Jeff hooted. "*Fifi!* What a wimp name!"

But then he took a good look at Fifi's face sticking out from under her cute, little dog hat and jumped back.

And then, to cover up how scared he was, he grabbed Bobby's crazy stocking

22

cap and tossed it to another kid. But Bobby chased the kid and got it back. So they all ran away up the street, chasing one another and grabbing each other's hats.

Mary Jo wanted to run after them and pelt them with snowballs, but I was sick of snowballs by then.

And besides, I still needed her to help me with the dogs.

By that time it was safe to pick up Fifi, so I cuddled her until she calmed down.

Then by the time we got to Mrs. Randolph's house (which is next to my apartment building), Fifi was all over being upset about the boys and the snowballs. But *I* was still mad.

Because of Bobby and his friends, we were late getting back, and Mrs. Randolph was watching for us from the window. I felt bad about her worrying. But mostly I

23

felt bad in case she would yell at me—which she didn't, thank goodness!

• • •

I hate it when people are mad at me. I don't know why Bobby likes to get in trouble so much.

If my father were still here, Bobby sure wouldn't *dare* get in trouble the way he does now.

One reason I am so mad at Bobby right now is that I can't tell on him. That's because when my mom gets home, we're supposed to go out for pizza and get our Christmas tree. And if I tell on Bobby, she might say we can't go.

• • •

Anyway, Mrs. Randolph didn't yell at me for getting Fifi back late, even though I could tell she was wondering what took so long. Of course, I didn't tell her that Bobby

24

threw snowballs at Fifi, or Mrs. Randolph would have had heart failure.

After we said good-bye to Fifi, Mary Jo and I went to drop off Patches.

Then I walked Mary Jo and Bruno back to their house, which is right next to the church.

Mary Jo and I talked about the Church Family Christmas Eve Party and what we were going to wear and how it was too bad that Julie Chang would have to miss it because her family is away on Christmas vacation.

Then Mary Jo walked me back to my apartment.

"Jeff and those boys are such goof heads," Mary Jo said. "Why does Bobby hang around with them?"

I wish I knew, God.

That's the way it was at our old school,

too. Bobby started hanging around with a bunch of kids who thought it was fun to get yelled at all the time.

Then we moved here so my mother could be closer to her sister, who is my Aunt Rosa. And that meant Bobby couldn't hang around with those old, wild kids anymore—which was good.

But now he hangs around with these *new,* wild kids.

●　　●　　●

Bobby came in just a little while ago, and this is what happened:

"Mom home yet?" he asked.

"No."

"So are you going to tell on me or what?"

"No."

"That's good, because you'd just better not."

"Listen here, Roberto!" I said. "I'm not

scared of you! The only reason I'm not telling about what you and your dopey friends did today is that Mom might change her mind about going out for pizza and getting the Christmas tree."

Bobby didn't argue with that. What could he say? That he hates pizza? He *loves* pizza! But he said, "My friends aren't dopey."

"Right," I said. "They're the smartest people in the world. It's *so intelligent* to throw snowballs at dogs, including a poor, little poodle."

"We weren't throwing snowballs at the *dogs!*" Bobby said, like he was mad I would even accuse him of doing such a rotten thing. "We were throwing snowballs at you and Mary Jo."

I had to admit that wasn't as bad. But *still!*

I couldn't think of anything more to say in the argument, and Bobby didn't say anything else, either. So probably it works out OK when two people get tired of arguing at the same time.

I like it better when Bobby and I don't fight. He can be lots of fun to play with, God, and sometimes he is very nice to me. The problem is, he likes to act like he's *a lot* older than I am when really he's only one year older. In fact, most of the time, people who don't know us think we are twins. That really drives Bobby crazy.

Before she left this morning, Mom said we could start unwrapping the Christmas ornaments today. So Bobby helped me get the box down from the shelf.

The ornaments and the figures for the Nativity set were all wrapped up in tissue paper from last year.

So Bobby and I played this game, God. We had to guess what was inside the tissue paper just by feeling it. Then we got to unwrap the ornament to see if we got it right.

My mother came home when we were almost finished, so she sat down and played the game with us.

Then I picked up a package, and I couldn't guess what it was. But when I opened it up, I saw it was the angel for the top of the Christmas tree. I had forgotten all about it. But as soon as I saw it again, I remembered going with my father last Christmas to buy it.

And then I started crying, God. I cried so hard it felt like my whole body was choking.

My mother scooped me up and rocked me like I was a little baby. She kept smoothing my hair and murmuring to me that everything was all right. But she was crying, too. And I was crying so hard I couldn't stop.

Bobby started yelling like he was really mad. "What's going on?" he said. "Why is Becky crying like that? Stop it! Stop it!"

Bobby jumped up and ran into his room and slammed the door.

"Why is Bobby mad at me?" I asked my

mother when I was finally able to talk.

"He's not angry, Becks," she said. "He's scared. Sometimes people sound mad when they're actually afraid. It's scary to see someone you love get so upset."

My mother got me a drink of water. Then she washed off my face and made me lie down on the couch with a blanket over me while she went to talk to Bobby.

●　●　●

Bobby came out a little while later, but we didn't say anything to each other.

I wasn't crying anymore. but I felt tired, and my head ached. I even felt embarrassed in a funny kind of way. Maybe Bobby felt embarrassed, too; I don't know.

Then my mother said that even though we were all feeling bad, it might be best to go ahead with our plans for pizza and the Christmas tree.

31

But Bobby said, "I don't want any dumb Christmas tree. They just stink up the house with that piney smell. And pizza makes me puke."

When he said that, God, I couldn't help it—I started giggling. And so did my mother.

Bobby scowled at us. But then his mouth started twitching. It was like his mouth wanted to laugh even if the rest of him didn't.

Finally his mouth won, and he laughed right out loud.

So we drove to the pizza place, and all the way there Bobby kept making pukey noises in the car. Finally my mother threatened to dump him headfirst into a snowbank.

LATER

Dear God,

Our tree is *so beautiful,* even though it is just a little one. We looked at a lot of trees, but that one seemed to be saying, "Oooo, Becky! Pick me! Pick me!" So I said to my mother, "How about this one?" And she and Bobby agreed with me that it was the best tree for us.

The tree is on our balcony for tonight, so its branches can spread out before we take it inside and decorate it. It's hard to wait. But I suppose having to wait can even be a good thing. Because that way, all the good stuff doesn't just happen to you at once. You keep having something to look forward to. That's why having Christmas Eve come before Christmas Day is a good idea.

Everything is very peaceful now, God.
The floodlight is shining on the angels.
And I just tore off today's link on my
countdown chain.

Good night, God.

Love,
Becky

December 20

Saturday

Dear God,

I woke up so happy this morning, and at first I couldn't tell why. Then I remembered that it was the first real day of Christmas vacation—hooray!

And then I saw the Christmas tree on the balcony and remembered that we are going to decorate it tonight after supper—hooray! Hooray!

● ● ●

But then at breakfast my mother gave us some bad news. She said she's worried about us being alone during the day when she's at work. Bobby and I are used to being alone after school until my mom gets home, but now she wanted to take us to Aunt Rosa's so we wouldn't be home alone all day.

But Bobby and I said, "Aw, Mom! No, come on, please? Not Aunt Rosa's! Please?"

Bobby said, "We'll be good. We promise."

And I said, "What about my dog-walking job? I can't do it on the other side of town. And there are no kids there to play with." (I wasn't counting my cousin, Yolanda, who is a lot older than Bobby and me. She plays the violin and is really good in math.)

Aunt Rosa isn't exactly mean, God, but she always makes you feel like you're in trouble for something. If you're not doing something, she tells you to do it. And if you *are* doing something, she tells you to

36

do something else. Like, she tells Bobby he should read and improve his mind. And she tells me that I read too much and I have an overactive imagination and that I should go outside and play.

● ● ●

For Christmas Aunt Rosa always gives me these math games like we have at school that no one plays with. The games are supposed to help you learn math. But the thing is, you have to be good in math to play the games in the first place. I hate math.

Of course, my mother makes me say thank you. But it's hard to mean it when you open up a present that you hope is going to be a new mystery book and it turns out to be some new kind of flash cards.

Aunt Rosa gives Bobby funny kinds of

presents, too. Like last year she gave him a long stocking cap that she knitted herself. It has all these bright colors and wild designs on it. I thought Bobby would really hate it. Maybe if it was just a *little* bit weird he would have hated it. But the cap is *so weird* that Bobby loved it right away. And he still loves it this winter as much as he did when he got it.

No other kid had one like it, that's for sure.

But even if Bobby likes his hat, he still doesn't like to stay at Aunt Rosa's house. It's like I said before, God. Aunt Rosa is not exactly mean, but a person can get real tired over there.

● ● ●

Well, good news, God! Mom worked things out with Mrs. Miller, who lives across the landing from us. Mrs. Miller is very nice, and she has these two cute, little kids my mom baby-sits sometimes. Every day that my mom isn't home, Bobby and I are supposed to eat lunch at Mrs. Miller's. The rest of the time, when we're not eating lunch, we're supposed to tell Mrs. Miller where we are. But it's up to us to be good on our own.

The rule is that we have to behave ourselves and stay in the neighborhood and do the list of housework jobs on the refrigerator door.

Before my mother left for work, she told us seven times to be good and that she would call us on her work breaks.

But if anything goes wrong—it's off to Aunt Rosa's!

LATER

Dear God,

I just tore off another link from my Christmas countdown chain. I suppose I should have waited until tonight, but it's so dark and gloomy out this afternoon, that it looks like nighttime. I even need the lights on, it's so dark.

It won't be many days now until Bobby, my mother, and I go to the Church Family Christmas Eve party. It's an Apple Street Church tradition, Mary Jo says, and it's supposed to be lots of fun.

After that, it will be Christmas morning. My mother will make pancakes, and the three of us will open our presents.

Then later we'll go over to Aunt Rosa's house for dinner, and there will be more presents from her. I think it's probably OK that my mother makes me say thank you, but I don't think I should have to look surprised when I get another math game, do you, God?

● ● ●

I heard Bobby tell Mrs. Miller he was going out sledding. But after I got done walking dogs, I told her I was going to stay inside where it was cozy and read my book.

● ● ●

I just saw the funniest thing, God! And my imagination isn't being overactive or anything. I saw this for sure.

There's a light on inside the church tower! I don't mean the floodlight for the angels; that's not turned on yet. But there's a light *in* the tower. There's this little window above the angels, and that's where the light is coming from. I wonder what it could be? I think I'll watch and see if it goes away.

41

It hasn't gone away yet. *Finally* something exciting and mysterious is happening around here. Maybe I should investigate it—like a real detective or something. But I sort of wish the light would just go out. It's making me too curious. And I get wiggly when I get too curious. Maybe I'll just read my book.

● ● ●

I keep trying to read my book, but I can't concentrate.

● ● ●

I decided to call Mary Jo.

When she answered the phone she said, "Bennett residence. M. J. Bennett here."

"*Mary Jo,*" I said. "There's a mysterious light on in the church tower. I can see it from my balcony window."

"Oooo, neat!" said Mary Jo. "Let's find out what's going on! Do you have a rope?"

42

"What do we need a rope for?" I asked. Sometimes Mary Jo makes me feel a little nervous.

Mary Jo sounded real excited. "We'll tie one around your balcony railing, right? Then we'll hold onto the other end. Then we'll jump off the balcony and swing across the street. At the other side, we'll grab onto an angel or something, and from there we'll climb into the tower, OK?"

I told Mary Jo we weren't allowed to play on the balcony like that. She sounded really disappointed. Then she said, "Oh, well. I guess we'll just have to use the stairs."

"What stairs?" I asked.

Then Mary Jo told me there's this little door inside the church that leads to a winding staircase, and the staircase leads to a little room up inside the tower. She

43

said the tower was just used for storing stuff—like the church Christmas decorations when they're not on display.

"But someone's up there now," I said.

"Yes," said Mary Jo. "Let's tiptoe up the stairs and take a peek. If it's a burglar, we can throw a net over him and tie him up."

"If it's a burglar, we should run away and call the police," I said.

Mary Jo was impatient to get going, I think. She said, "Well, that might work, too. We can make up our minds when we get there."

● ● ●

I called out to Mrs. Miller that I was going to the church to play with Mary Jo. I pulled on my coat as I ran across the street. I was shivering, but I couldn't tell which shivers were from being cold and which ones were from being fun-scared.

44

Mary Jo led the way to a little door in the corner of the sanctuary. It was unlocked, and when we opened it, we saw a narrow staircase winding up and up. It was just like the kind of stairs you read about in mystery books about haunted castles.

Mary Jo remembered to bring a flashlight, which was smart of her. I wished I was the one who thought of it. Detectives are supposed to have flashlights, and magnifying glasses, too, I think. Oh, well.

The light was on in the stairway, but we still used the flashlight, too, since it was more fun.

Mary Jo put her finger up to her lips in a *shhh* sign and started up the stairs. I followed right behind her. Maybe I should have gone first, since I was the one who saw the light. But Mary Jo was the one

45

who knew about the stairs. So it worked out fine.

The stairs made little, creaky noises when we stepped on them, but we tried to be very, very quiet.

The door was open at the landing at the top of the stairs. We could see a light, and we could hear someone moving around.

We tiptoed over to the door and peeked into the dusty, little room. We tried not to make a sound. We saw a man with his back to us. He was digging through some boxes, and there were piles of yellow, crumbly papers all around him.

"OH, NO!" said Mary Jo right out loud. "It's only *Daddy*!"

Pastor Bennett jumped up so fast he just about fell over. He pressed his hand on his chest to make his heart stop beating so fast.

46

"*Mary Jo*! You startled me! How can the world's noisiest kid sneak up on anyone?"

Mary Jo flopped down on a little stool. "Becky saw the light from her balcony window. We thought you were a ghost. Or a monster. Or at least a burglar!" She sounded like someone who gets all set to go ice-skating and then finds out the lake isn't frozen.

Pastor Bennett smiled at us. He was still trying to catch his breath. "Sorry to disappoint you, girls."

Well, I guess I was a *little* disappointed, God, but to tell you the truth, I was mostly *glad* it was only Pastor Bennett. I didn't know where Mary Jo was going to get a net to throw over a burglar.

I walked over to the window and looked out. I was right above the angel with the trumpet. It was wonderful to see them up close like that. The floodlight was shining in my eyes a little bit, but I could still look across the street and see my own balcony window.

Pastor Bennett said, "Actually, I'm working on a little mystery of my own that might interest you two."

I turned away from the window, pulled up a box, and sat down beside Mary Jo. A real, live mystery!

● ● ●

Here is what Pastor Bennett told us, God. He said one of the long-ago pastors at Apple Street Church was also a famous hymn writer. Pastor Bennett collects old books, and last week he found a journal that Pastor Kirkland, this hymn writer, has written years and years ago.

"Like the prayer journals Miss Jenkins told us we could write?" I asked.

"Yes," said Pastor Bennett. "Like that. Well, the interesting thing is that, in his journal, Pastor Kirkland mentions that he wrote *a Christmas song* for his wife to sing at the Christmas Eve service."

"You mean like the Christmas Eve service we *still* have?" I asked.

"Right again!" Pastor Bennett said. "It's an Apple Street tradition."

"What song is it?" Mary Jo asked. "Can you sing it, Daddy?"

"No, that's just it. I can't," said Pastor Bennett. "I don't think anyone ever got to hear the song."

"How come?" I asked.

"Well, that's where the mystery comes in, Becky. According to Pastor Kirkland's journal, he wrote the song in the summertime. He wanted to give the song to his wife on her birthday, which was just before

50

Christmas. His idea was that she could sing it in church on Christmas Eve.

"But Pastor Kirkland could never keep a secret. So he gave the sheet of music to his little girl, Anna, and told her to hide it where her mother wouldn't find it. And where he wouldn't find it either! It was a kind of game. Only Anna would know where the music was until it came time for her mother's birthday.

"But a couple of months later, the journal becomes very sad, because that autumn Anna got very sick and died."

We were all very quiet for a long time, thinking about Anna and her mother and father.

Then I said, "Didn't her parents ever find the song?"

Pastor Bennett shook his head. "Anna's father never mentioned it again in his

51

journal. Maybe it made him too sad to think about the games he and Anna played.

"I don't think anyone ever found the music. I know all of Pastor Kirkland's hymns, and none of them seems to be the Christmas one he describes in his journal. Maybe he or his wife came across the music eventually, but I don't think so. I think it's still in the place where their little girl, Anna, hid it all those years ago."

"Is that what you were looking for up here?" Mary Jo asked.

Pastor Bennett sighed. "Well, I thought I'd give it a try. All sorts of old stuff has accumulated in this room over the years. And if I found the music, it would be nice to play it at this year's Christmas Eve service. But I didn't find any songs. I did find a picture of Anna, though."

Mary Jo and I jumped up at the same time. "Where? Where?" we asked.

Pastor Bennett showed us an old, old photograph. It was a little bit blurry, but it was Apple Street Church in the background all right! We could even see the window of the tower where we were sitting right that minute. (That gave me a kind of funny feeling, God, to think of my church being around a long time before I was born. But it was a kind of nice feeling, too.)

In the picture, Anna was standing in front of the church. She was holding a cute dog. And I knew the minute I saw her that if I had lived back then, Anna and I would have been good friends. Don't ask me how I knew. I just did.

As I looked at Anna's picture, I wanted to ask her, "Where did you hide the Christmas song, Anna?" I could tell just from

53

looking at her that she would have picked an excellent spot. Her face had a kind of laughing, fun look—and she looked smart, too.

We were all thinking hard about Anna and the lost Christmas song when suddenly we heard a noise outside—a kind of thud-splat, thud-splat.

"What could that be?" asked Pastor Bennett.

The three of us rushed to the window and looked out.

●   ●   ●

The noise was coming from a bunch of boys on the ground below. They had sleds with them, and they were throwing snowballs at the sheep decorations.

Bobby was one of the kids. As usual, he was wearing his crazy hat.

Pastor Bennett dashed downstairs and

54

caught the boys before they managed to get away. It looked like he was making them tell him who they were.

"What a goof head thing for those boys to do!" exclaimed Mary Jo. "I bet Daddy talks to their parents!"

I nodded, but I was too miserable and embarrassed to say anything.

LATER

Dear God,

My mother couldn't believe how quiet Bobby and I were at supper. I'm pretty sure she could guess something was wrong, but neither Bobby or I wanted to say anything about the snowballs.

Then, after supper, Pastor Bennett called to ask my mother if he could come over and talk to her and Bobby.

● ● ●

Pastor Bennett sounded like a father. He was very nice as usual, but he also sounded very firm.

He said Bobby and the other boys probably didn't think throwing snowballs at the sheep was that big a deal. But he said that it was really vandalism and he didn't want to hear about it happening again.

Bobby said he was sorry, and it sounded

56

to me like he really meant it. He said he hadn't thought it was so bad because they weren't throwing snowballs at the shepherds or anything—just the sheep. Then he said that some of the kids wanted to throw snowballs at the angels but that he had talked them out of it.

My mother told me before Pastor Bennett came over that I wasn't supposed to say a word, because this was Bobby's problem. But when Bobby said that about the angels, I couldn't help myself, God.

I yelled, "Those kids wanted to do WHAT? They'd better leave those angels alone, is all I've got to say!"

I think my mother was going to send me to my room, but just then the phone rang and I went to answer it. It was old Mrs. Randolph, but she wasn't calling to talk to me about Fifi. She wanted to talk to my mother, and it turned out she wanted to complain about Bobby again. She saw the kids throwing snowballs at the sheep, and she recognized Bobby by his wild stocking cap.

My mother told her she'd already heard from Pastor Bennett and that the problem had been taken care of.

I think Mom was kind of annoyed with Mrs. Randolph for calling and complaining again. But for some reason, being mad at Mrs. Randolph seemed to make my mother even madder at Bobby. She said to him, "What kind of home will people think you come from?"

Bobby said he would be good from now on and stop messing around with Jeff and the other boys. My mother said that was fine, but Bobby is still grounded for all day tomorrow. He can go to Sunday school and church, but that's it.

LATER
Dear God,
It took my mother a little while to get over being mad at Bobby. He is still grounded, but at least my mother isn't mad at him anymore.

So we set up the tree and decorated it. We played Christmas music on the record player and drank hot chocolate with those little marshmallows in it.

The music reminded me of Pastor Kirkland's Christmas song that his daughter, Anna, hid.

So I told my mother and Bobby all about Pastor Bennett's super-good mystery, and they were very interested. I told them how

Mary Jo and I had been detectives when we investigated the light in the tower that turned out to be only Pastor Bennett hunting through papers. I said I wanted to keep on being a detective and find the lost Christmas song so Pastor Bennett can sing it on Christmas Eve.

LATER

Dear God,

I am writing this while I'm looking out of my balcony window at the angels. The floodlight is shining on them, and they look very peaceful and pretty.

I'm glad the boys didn't throw snowballs at them. That would have been a terrible thing to do. It was bad enough for the poor sheep. So what if Bobby says they didn't throw snowballs at the shepherds? I don't think people should throw snowballs at

60

animals *or* people. And certainly not at angels.

● ● ●

Sometimes, God, when I'm thinking about something, I can't go to sleep. It's like my brain is a machine that won't do what I tell it to. There's no little switch where I can just turn it off.

First of all, I started thinking about Anna Kirkland.

And then I started thinking about getting a dog.

Anna's father reminded me of my own father. My father couldn't keep secrets, either. He always had to do his Christmas shopping at the very last minute, because if the presents were hidden in the house, he would end up giving them to people when it wasn't even Christmas yet!

If my father were here this Christmas, I

61

think he would get me a dog. That would sure be a hard present to hide! But I think he would be proud of me because of my dog-walking job. Maybe he would figure I was old enough to take care of my own dog.

But I don't know if my mother will think that way. I told her I wanted a dog, but she has a lot on her mind. And maybe a dog isn't one of the big things on her mind. Or maybe it's not on her mind at all.

I could tell by Anna's picture that she liked dogs. I wonder if the dog she is holding in the picture is her own or just one she borrowed?

I bet her father and mother were very sad when Anna got sick and died. I wonder if it feels the same way to grown-ups when their children die as it does to kids when their parents die. Like, I wonder if Pastor Kirkland or Mrs. Kirkland ever just happened to see one of Anna's toys or hair ribbons—the way I found the Christmas tree angel my father and I bought. If they found something of Anna's, did it make them cry so hard they thought they'd never stop?

Anyway, I think Anna's father was a lot like mine. If my father wrote a Christmas song for my mom, he would probably tell me to hide it in a good place.

So where would I hide it? I wonder if I would think of the same place Anna did?

This is a good case for me to work on, isn't it, God? Maybe you could help my brain work extra well so I can solve my case in time for Christmas Eve.

Love,
Becky

Glory to God in the Highest

December 21

Sunday

Dear God,

We just got home from church a little while ago, and Bobby can't go out again—because of the snowballs he threw at the sheep yesterday.

I am writing this with a pencil, because Bobby just made me give him his pen back.

I think he did that because he's mad that I'm not grounded and he is.

My mother doesn't work on Sundays. But her store just called and asked her to come in because one of the other salesladies went home with a high fever.

My mother put Bobby *on his honor* to stay grounded while she's away. She didn't have time to take him to Aunt Rosa's, and the Millers aren't home.

Bobby will *really* be on his honor, because even I won't be here. My Sunday school class is going over to Miss Jenkins's house to wrap Christmas presents for poor kids. Mary Jo and I will be the only girls there, because Julie is on vacation. But the boys will be Danny Petrowski, Pug McConnell, and Curtis Anderson. They are all real nice.

LATER
Dear God,

I thought Bobby would stay grounded, and then everything would be all right.

But, instead, the most terrible thing happened! Wait till I tell you!

Miss Jenkins dropped me off a little bit before my mom got home. The first thing I did was go to the window to take a look at the angels. I wondered why the floodlight wasn't on yet, even though it was getting dark.

But then just after my mother got home, the *police* came to talk to her!

They said someone *stole the floodlight* from the church and that it was probably the same kids who have been causing lots of other trouble lately.

"And you think my son is involved?" asked my mother.

"Could be," said the policeman. "Someone called about the kids and said Bobby was one of them."

"But I wasn't!" Bobby cried. "I didn't have anything to do with it! I didn't even know they were going to do that!"

"The caller recognized you by your stocking cap," said the policeman.

"No!" cried Bobby, sounding really scared. "I don't even have that hat anymore. One of the kids took it!"

"Which one?" asked the other policeman.

"I-I don't know," said Bobby. "It happened kind of fast."

"When did this happen?" they asked.

"This afternoon." Bobby mumbled so quietly we could hardly hear him.

My mother looked at him like she could hardly believe her ears. But she didn't say anything, with the policemen still there.

Bobby seemed really scared, and so was I. But then this really important question popped up in my head, and I knew I had to ask it out loud. My voice came out all soft and squeaky, but I asked, "Did you get the floodlight back?"

The police looked kind of surprised when I said that, because I'd been kind of scrunched up in the corner of the couch. Maybe they didn't even see me there at first. Maybe it sounded like a pillow talking.

But they answered me. "No, we've questioned the boys we think are involved, but

68

we haven't recovered the floodlight. They may have hidden it. Or—they may just have thrown it away. We don't know why they would have stolen it in the first place."

I don't know either, God.

The policemen gave Bobby a stern warning and left.

● ● ●

My mother was madder than I ever saw her before.

She said to Bobby, "You gave me your *word* that you would stay inside and serve your punishment. And you go out—out STEALING?"

Bobby started to cry. "But I didn't *do* it!"

I spoke up. "I bet you anything it was Mrs. Randolph who called the police when she saw the boys over at the church. She

69

doesn't see that well. But maybe she recognized Bobby's hat. And she didn't know it was another kid wearing it."

"YES!" said Bobby before my mother could tell me to keep out of this. "She must have thought one of those other kids was me. One of the kids took my hat—I told you that."

"I would like to hear more about that, Roberto!" said my mother. "How could anyone steal your hat if you were *inside where you were supposed to be?*"

Right away Bobby looked like he wished he hadn't said anything. But he probably figured he had to get in a *little bit* of trouble about the hat so he could stay out of *big trouble* about the floodlight.

He said, "Uh, well. Some of the guys sort of came over this afternoon. I told them I couldn't come out, but they couldn't hear

70

me well enough. So I sort of went outside to talk to them. And I told them I couldn't hang around with them anymore. No, really, I did!

"But they started goofing around, and one of them grabbed my hat. I yelled at them, but they ran away.

"And that's all I know! I didn't help them take the floodlight. I didn't even know they were going to do it. I don't even know why they wanted it."

Bobby opened the clothes closet and pointed to the empty hook. "See?" he said. "No hat!"

"And you weren't over by the church?" asked my mother.

Bobby looked at the floor. "No," he said.

My mother looked really tired. She wasn't yelling anymore, but I think she was still upset with Bobby. She said, "All right, Roberto. I'm going to take you at your word again. I believe you when you say that you weren't involved in stealing the floodlight. But I'm very angry that you were with those kids again today. You were supposed to stay inside, and you went out. Tomorrow you're grounded at Aunt Rosa's."

Bobby opened his mouth to say something. But then I guess he figured it wouldn't be such a good idea.

My mother sent us *both* to bed super-early.

● ● ●

So this turned out to be a pretty awful day, God.

I just tore off another link from my Christmas countdown chain. At least Christmas is coming. And at least Christmas Eve is coming even sooner.

72

But the *bad* part about Christmas Eve coming so soon is that I don't have much time to find the sheet of music Anna hid.

From my bed in the old dining room I can hear the refrigerator start up. And I can hear the funny clanking noises the heater makes. They don't scare me.

But it would still be nicer if I could look out and see the angels. I can see them a *little* bit with the light from the streetlamp. But it's not the same as with the floodlight; I miss seeing my angels all lit up.

I think it's really bad when people take things, God! Why do people do things like that? Now the angels won't even be lit up on Christmas Eve unless the people at church buy a new light right away. Or unless someone finds the old light and gets it back.

I just got an idea, God! Maybe *I* could do that! Maybe I could find the floodlight! I don't know how yet, but maybe I will think of something.

Do you know what this is like? It's like I'm a real detective, and I'm working on *two* cases:

CASE NUMBER 1: Find the Christmas song Anna Kirkland hid a long time ago.

CASE NUMBER 2: Find out what happened to the floodlight and get it back if I can.

I have to solve both my cases by Christmas Eve, God. I don't have much time.

Love,
Becky

December 22

Monday

Dear God,

I woke up excited this morning, and at first I couldn't remember why. Then I thought of my two detective cases. I used to think nothing mysterious or exciting ever happened around here, and now look! Before I had *zero* cases, and now I have *two*.

I told Bobby this at breakfast. But he wasn't real nice about it. He said, "Oh, I'm so sure. Just like you're a real detective or something."

"Well, it could happen," I said. "I could

75

find something that's been lost. Besides, how do you know so much about it? You never even *tried* to be a detective."

Bobby looked at me kind of funny, but he didn't say anything. I figured he was mad that I got to go out and solve cases and he had to be cooped up inside with Yolanda, who plays the violin.

I don't think Bobby would say being a detective is a dumb idea if he could be one. I wish he could stay home with me and be my partner. Even if he isn't in a very good mood! It's a good thing I didn't tell him to have a nice day, because he might have hit me.

● ● ●

My mother and Bobby left a little while ago. So now I've got to figure out how to be a detective.

I know I've got to look for clues.

76

And I think it would be good if I had a bloodhound.

But there isn't a bloodhound on my dog-walking job, so I'll just have to use the smartest one—which is Fifi, of all people! She's crabby, but she's not dumb. I don't think many detective dogs wear little boots and doggy sweaters, but what can I do?

LATER

Dear God,

When I went to get Fifi this afternoon, Mrs. Randolph started talking about Bobby again.

I took a deep breath and told her that someone took Bobby's hat and that's why people might think he was with the kids who stole the floodlight, but he wasn't.

Mrs. Randolph looked surprised and just

said, "Oh!" So I don't know whether she believed what Bobby said or not.

But *I* believe him, God! I just wish I could prove for sure that Bobby wasn't even at the church yesterday when the floodlight was taken.

I decided to start working on my cases over at the church. I thought I might find a clue about where the floodlight was. I thought maybe I could follow footprints or something.

Besides, I thought being at the church would give me an idea about where Anna hid the Christmas song.

● ● ●

But when Fifi and I got to the shepherd display, we saw that the ground was all trampled, and we couldn't figure out which footprints to follow.

Fifi started digging around, but all she

78

found were some rocks and twigs and old, dead leaves.

Then she picked up something that looked like a twig—only it was blue. I told Fifi to give it to me, which she didn't want to do at first. Maybe she thought it was a toy. But I could tell Fifi wasn't in a bad mood. So I gently opened her mouth and made her give the blue thing to me.

It turned out to be a pen like the kind Bobby's teacher gave her class for Christmas. I knew those kinds of pens sometimes had kids' names printed on them. So I turned it over to see.

It had a name on it all right. ROBERTO GARCIA, JR.

● ● ●

I couldn't believe it, God!

I wanted to find some good proof, but all I found was bad proof instead.

"Thanks a lot, Fifi!" I said. But I knew I couldn't get mad at her when she was only doing her job.

I thought about digging a hole in the snow and putting the pen back. I thought maybe I could pretend I never found it in the first place. But I wasn't sure a good detective was allowed to do that. Besides, someone *else* might find the pen and figure out that Bobby had been there.

I also thought about just throwing the pen away in a garbage can. But I didn't think I could do that, since it didn't belong to me.

So I figured I would show it to Bobby and tell him I *knew* he was lying. Even though I believed him at first.

LATER

Dear God,

After supper, Bobby and I had to do the dishes like we always do. I thought that would be a good time to talk to him alone.

I whispered to him so my mother couldn't hear from the next room.

I said, "Bobby, you didn't tell the truth about not being with those kids when they stole the light. And I can prove it!"

Bobby almost dropped a dish. "WHAT? You're crazy!" he said.

I said, "Be quiet! Unless you want Mom to hear you, that is."

Bobby said, "What are you *talking* about?" He sounded really upset, but at least he whispered like he was supposed to.

"I went looking for clues by the church, and look what I found!" I held out the pen.

82

"Give it back!" Bobby tried to grab it out of my hand, but the pen fell in the dishwater.

"Now look what you did!" I said.

My mother called from the living room, "What's going on in there?"

"Nothing!" Bobby and I called out together. Then we gave each other mean looks.

I fished the pen out of the dishwater. I said, "You had your pen on Sunday, because you made me give it back. But you didn't drop it when we went to church, because that was before. It was still in my room then. So how did it get over by the church, is what I'd like to know."

"That's what I'd like to know, too," said my mother from the doorway.

Bobby and I both jumped. I guess we had been whispering louder than we thought.

My mother wasn't yelling, but she almost sounded *too* calm, if you know what I mean, God. I knew Bobby was in even bigger trouble than before.

My mother held out her hand for the pen, so I had to give it to her.

"Bobby," she said. "I specifically asked you if you had gone over to the church yesterday, and you said *no*."

Bobby stared at the floor. "I know I said that. I *was* over by the church, Mom. But not for the reason you think. I was afraid to tell you, because I thought you'd get mad at me."

"Well, you got that one right," said my mother.

"I got bored being grounded," he said.

"Grounding is *supposed* to be boring," said my mother. "It wouldn't be much of a punishment if it weren't, would it?"

"I guess not," Bobby said in a little voice. Then he tried to explain. "I—well, I sort of figured it would be fun to be a detective, like Becky's doing. I mean, I figured if she could do it, I could do it even better, since I'm so much older. So I went to the church to see if I could find out anything about the song that Anna girl hid. I took my pen and some paper, because detectives are supposed to make notes and stuff. But I must have dropped the pen. Anyway, I *wasn't* with those kids when they stole the light. The light was *still there* when I was looking around. Honest!"

"*Honest!*" said my mother. "*Honest*?? Bobby, why should I believe you're being honest about anything anymore? You broke your grounding *twice* yesterday when you gave me your word that I could trust you to obey. You lied to me when I asked you if you were at the church. So why should I believe you now when you say you didn't have anything to do with the stolen light? No, I'm sorry, Bobby. I have had it! I was going to let you stay home tomorrow, but tomorrow you go back to Aunt Rosa's."

Bobby started to whine, because he said Aunt Rosa made him clean house all day long and he was only allowed to watch educational TV and he had to listen to Yolanda take her violin lesson.

I don't know if everything he told us was *exactly* true, but he didn't have a very nice day.

Then my mother sent us *both* to bed even though it was still super-early.

"Thanks a lot, Becky," Bobby said to me. "I thought you were supposed to be the Great Detective who was helping me. And now look at all the trouble I'm in."

● ● ●

That made me feel really awful, God. The funny part is, I really *believe* Bobby when he says he was just hunting for clues yesterday.

You know what? I think the only thing I can do about it is to hunt for more proof. I hope it turns out to be good proof—not bad.

87

● ● ●

If I look real hard out my window, I can still see my angels. The one with the banner. The one playing the trumpet. And the one playing the cymbals.

I sure miss the floodlight! Things don't always work out exactly right, do they, God? Like, I don't think Anna Kirkland really meant to hide the music so well that no one would ever find it.

I keep asking myself, If I were Anna, where would I put it? Under the bed? In a closet? In a drawer?

But none of those places seems good enough.

In the pocket of my doll's dress? Taped under my dog's food dish? In my Bible?

Maybe Anna hid it in the little tower room? Except Pastor Bennett and Mary Jo and I have looked all through there. It's

88

too bad Bobby has to go back to Aunt Rosa's tomorrow, or I could show him the tower room. I think he would like it.

I bet Anna went up in the tower room sometimes. It's funny to think of her going up the same steps Mary Jo and I climbed when I first saw the light in the tower.

● ● ●

Well, I'm getting a little tired of thinking about all this, God. So I will tear a link off my Christmas countdown chain and go to sleep.

● ● ●

But I just thought of something I want to ask you, God. Can the people who went to Apple Street Church a long, long time ago still belong to the church family even if they are dead? I mean, can people who are on earth and people who are in heaven still belong to each other?

89

Because, in that way, Anna could kind of be my friend, even though I never met her. Do people all know each other in heaven? Does my father know Anna?

Well, anyway, tell both of them I said "hi."

Love,
Becky

December 23

Tuesday

Dear God,

If you think Bobby was in a bad mood yesterday when he had to go to Aunt Rosa's, you should have seen him this morning.

He was mostly in a bad mood at me, because I'm the one who found the pen that got him in trouble. But, of course, Bobby's the one who dropped the pen in the first place. So he really got his own self in trouble. But I'm afraid that doesn't stop him being mad at me.

So there you have it, God. My mother is

still mad at Bobby. And Bobby is still mad at me.

My mother and Bobby just left, and I am feeling very lonely, God.

●　　●　　●

Well, I just got some good news that might help me not to be so lonely for a while. Mrs. Miller from across the landing asked if I would play with her little kids while she's doing Christmas stuff like baking cookies and cleaning the house. I asked her if Mary Jo could come help me, and she said, "Sure."

So I called Mary Jo, and she came running, which is about the only way that Mary Jo gets places.

●　　●　　●

We had a really good time playing with the little kids, God. One of them is three, and the other one is one and a half.

92

We took them out and showed them how to make a snowman in the front yard. They liked it a lot, but they weren't much help, so Mary Jo and I had to do most of the work.

Then we showed them how to make snow angels. First, you have to find a good patch of snow that isn't all messed up already. Then you lie down on your back and wave your arms and legs in the snow. When you get up, you can see a kind of angel-picture. Your legs made the angel's robe, and your arms made the angel's wings.

The little kids' angels didn't turn out too well, but we didn't tell them that. We said they did a good job—which I guess they did, when you think about how little they are.

Making the angels in the snow reminded me of the angels on the tower and the floodlight that was gone.

That happens to me sometimes, God. I'll be going along, having a fun time, and then I'll remember something *yucky*. And then it feels as if someone hit me in the chest with a giant snowball or something. *Thud!*

So anyway, after we helped the little kids make a snowman and angels, we took them for a little sled ride.

Then it was time for us to go in for lunch. As part of lunch, Mrs. Miller gave us hot chocolate and Christmas cookies, so that was nice.

Then it was time for the little kids' naps. I read them some Christmas stories to get them to go to sleep, and they liked that a lot.

Then Mary Jo had to go home and help

95

her mother, and I went back to my own apartment to read mysteries until it was time for my dog-walking job.

Then it felt like another snowball hit me in the chest, because reading about mysteries made me think that I haven't done very well on my two cases yet.

I didn't find the floodlight and prove Bobby didn't steal it. (Just the opposite! I found proof that made it seem like Bobby was there after all.)

And on top of all that, I didn't find the song that Anna Kirkland hid.

I remember yesterday I said I was going to look for more clues today. But I don't have any good ideas about how to do that.

● ● ●

I was still feeling bad about all that when I went to pick up Fifi Randolph and Patches Johnson. Usually they make me feel good right away, because I like dogs so much. But this time they just reminded me that I don't have a dog of my own—and who knows? Maybe I never will. At least not while I'm still a kid.

Patches and Fifi knew right away that I was feeling sad. Dogs are funny like that. They just know. Anyway, they were both really sweet to me, and that made me feel better.

Then I saw Mary Jo running toward us with Bruno. That made me feel better, too. It's hard to be quiet and sad when Mary Jo is around. It would be like trying to be quiet and sad on a roller coaster.

So we set off walking the dogs. I took Bruno, and Mary Jo took Patches and Fifi.

Everything was going OK until we turned a corner. And suddenly the biggest clue yet popped up—right in front of me.

"Mary Jo!" I said, trying not to talk too loud. "Look at that boy up ahead!"

"What about him?" Mary Jo asked.

"His hat!" I said. "Look at his hat! It's not his—it's Bobby's! He's wearing *Bobby's* hat! That proves Bobby was telling the truth about someone taking it. So it *wasn't* Bobby Mrs. Randolph saw stealing the floodlight—it was another kid!"

Mary Jo looked at me like she couldn't listen as fast as I was talking.

"*Bobby* stole the floodlight??" she asked.

"No, no, no. Bobby *didn't* steal the floodlight. People think he did, but he didn't. Come on, we've got to follow that kid and see where he goes!"

For once Mary Jo was hurrying to catch up with me. "What are you going to do?" she asked, trying to catch her breath.

Well, to tell you the truth, God, I hadn't thought about that.

"I don't know," I said. "Just follow that hat!"

•   •   •

We tried to follow like they do on TV. We didn't want to get too close, because then he might see us. But we didn't want to stay too far back in case we lost him.

A couple of times we thought for sure he was going to turn around. So we tried real hard to look like we were just a couple of kids walking some dogs.

But he didn't turn around or notice us, so we followed him all the way to Jeff's house. He didn't go up to the front door. Instead he went around to the garage, which was at the other end of the back-yard, next to the alley.

Mary Jo and I decided to peek in the window and see what was going on.

As we were coming up to the garage, all of a sudden it looked like a million lights were switched on inside.

Mary Jo and I looked at each other at the same exact minute. "The floodlight!" we said together.

"But why would they have it in the garage?" asked Mary Jo. "Do people need that bright a light to work on their cars?"

"I don't think so," I said, trying to figure it out as I was talking. "Because then *everybody* would need a floodlight. Let's look in the window."

So we told Fifi, Bruno, and Patches to be quiet. I don't think they knew what was going on. They were just happy to be getting an extra-long walk.

When we tiptoed up to the window and

looked in, we could see that there weren't just regular kids in there. There were teenagers, too.

One of them was Jeff's brother, and the big kids had musical instruments, like for a band. The floodlight was tied up high on the ceiling, shining down on them.

They were getting ready to play, and the younger kids were just sort of hanging around, watching and listening to the older ones.

I saw Jeff, and I heard him say to his big brother, "Hey, Rick. Do you like the spotlight I got for you, Rick? Huh?"

I don't know why, but I got the feeling Jeff had asked Rick that a zillion times.

Rick said, "Yeah, yeah, yeah. It's great. Now shut up so we can practice." Then he turned to the other teenagers and said, "One, two, three . . ."

And the *second* they started to play, Patches threw back his head and *howled*. I don't know whether it hurt his ears or whether he just thought he was singing along. Then Bruno started barking and jumping around. And even Fifi went *yip-yip-yip-yip* in her crabbiest voice.

The dogs made so much noise you could hear them over the band. But the band sounded so TERRIBLE, who wouldn't bark?!?

As soon as the boys heard the dogs, they looked up and saw us spying on them. So they started running toward the door. We wanted to get out of there fast, but Fifi had other ideas!

She broke loose from Mary Jo and ran right at the boys as they came tumbling out of the garage. (I think she recognized them as the kids who threw snowballs at

us. Like I said before, God, Fifi's not dumb, but she *is* crabby.)

She jumped straight up and grabbed Bobby's hat in her teeth and pulled it right off that kid's head!

"Hey!" yelled the kid, which was probably all he could think of to say.

Then Fifi took off running up the alley with that hat in her mouth.

"Get Fifi! Please!" I said to Mary Jo. "Catch her!" I was so afraid Fifi would go out in the street and get run over.

Mary Jo took off like a rocket, and I turned to go after her. The boys started chasing me, but just then Bruno and Patches got in their way, because the dogs thought we were all just playing a fun game. The boys fell over the dogs and landed in a big, clumsy pile.

So I grabbed Bruno and Patches and got away.

I ran so hard and fast I got a stitch in my side, and I couldn't see Mary Jo or Fifi anywhere. I was afraid I'd lost them.

But then I saw one of Fifi's little boots in the snow. And farther ahead I saw another one. She must have run so fast they dropped off her feet. I kept following the next two boots, and finally I caught up with Fifi and Mary Jo.

Fifi's leash had gotten tangled in a bush, and Mary Jo was trying to get it undone. But when I came up she said, "Here! You do this!" And she plopped right down in the snow. That's the first time I ever saw Mary Jo collapse like that. "Dumb poodle!" I heard her mumble.

Fifi still had Bobby's hat in her mouth,

but I figured this wouldn't be the best time to try and get it away from her.

"We've got to tell your dad where the floodlight is," I said, when I had enough breath to talk.

Mary Jo jumped up. "Right! Let's go!"

But I suddenly realized how late it was. "No, you'd better go on without me. I have to get Patches and Fifi home. I'll come over later, OK?"

"OK!" said Mary Jo. She was already halfway across the street.

Mrs. Randolph was standing on the porch looking up and down the street when Fifi and I came up. She started to yell at me for being late and for not keeping Fifi's boots on her. But then she wanted to know about the hat Fifi had in her mouth. (It still wasn't a good time to take it away from her.)

106

I told Mrs. Randolph the whole story and about how Fifi was a heroine for getting Bobby's hat back. That just about gave her heart failure, but I could tell she was proud of Fifi, too. And she said, "So Bobby wasn't wearing the hat when I saw the boys steal the floodlight! Well, what do you know!"

Then she said, "I'm sorry I accused Bobby."

"I'll tell him," I said.

Then the two of us talked to Fifi for a while, and finally she gave me the hat. If you want to know the truth, God, I think she just got tired of holding it.

● ● ●

When Bobby and my mother got home and saw the hat, their eyes just about popped out of their heads. So I had to tell the whole story all over again. But that

107

was OK, because it was a good story.

And just as I was finishing, the floodlight went on at church, shining on the angels.

"They got the light back!" I cried. "Come on, let's go!"

I grabbed my coat and ran out the door with my mother and Bobby following me.

● ● ●

The floodlight was stuck back in the ground where it belonged, and a whole bunch of people were standing around it. I saw the janitor, Mr. Jones, and some neighbors and, of course, Mary Jo and Pastor Bennett. Mrs. Bennett even brought Mary Jo's baby brother, Matthew, outside to see all the excitement.

"Here's our girl!" said Pastor Bennett as soon as I came up. "Good detective work, Becky! Mary Jo told me how you tracked down the light. Sounds like you had a pretty exciting afternoon!"

His words made me feel warm all over. It was like drinking a gallon of hot chocolate and feeling warm all the way to my fingers and toes. He was so nice to say that! But it made me wish I could have found Anna's song, too. That would have made everything doubly nice. But at least the angels were lit up now and Bobby was out of trouble.

I kept looking up at the beautiful angels. I looked at them one at a time. At the one holding the banner. At the one playing the cymbals. At the one playing the trumpet.

And suddenly I knew.

I don't know how.

But I positively knew.

"Pastor Bennett," I said, my voice coming out all soft and squeaky. "Pastor Bennett. I know where Anna Kirkland hid the Christmas song."

"What?" he asked. "How do you know?"

I said, "I guessed. I guessed where Anna hid it. Those angels have been around for a long time, right? Even when Anna was a little girl? And when it's not Christmas, they're kept in the tower room, right? Well, Anna could have gone up there—just like Mary Jo and I did. And even though her father wrote the song in the summer, Anna would have wanted to hide it in a Christmasy place, I bet. And I bet she wanted to hide it in a musicky place, too. If I had been Anna, that's how I would have figured out where to hide it. So we have to take the angel down. The one with the trumpet."

Pastor Bennett had been listening hard to me. "Honey, it's a lot of work to take the

110

angel down . . ." he started to say.

Then Mary Jo said, *"Please,* Daddy! Becky thinks Anna rolled up the song and hid it in the angel's trumpet. Right, Becky? Right? Right??" She was jumping up and down, she was so excited.

"Hey, yeah!" Bobby said. "Yeah. The trumpet. Why didn't I think of that?"

Pastor Bennett said to the janitor, "Mr. Jones, will you get the ladder out, please?"

Mr. Jones grumbled that this was the craziest thing he ever did hear of, but he went to get the super-long ladder.

Mary Jo wanted to be the one to climb up it, but her mother wouldn't let her. Instead, Pastor Bennett, Mr. Jones, and some of the neighbors worked together to take the angel down off the tower and lay it on the ground.

It had to be a kid who reached into the

trumpet, because a grown-up's arm wouldn't fit. Pastor Bennett picked me.

I took off my mitten and reached my hand into the trumpet. I was so excited I was shaking.

But my fingers didn't touch anything.

"It's—it's not there!" I said. I could feel myself starting to cry. I had been so *sure*. And now I felt so embarrassed I wanted to run away.

Just then Bobby spoke up. "Maybe you didn't reach far enough, Becks. Maybe Anna poked it way up inside so it wouldn't fall out. What we need is a pair of tongs. You know—like for a barbeque or something."

"Tongs!" cried Mary Jo. "Gotcha!" And she took off running toward her house. She was back with the tongs in a second, but it seemed to me that it took forever.

112

Pastor Bennett took the tongs Mary Jo gave him and poked them into the trumpet.

"I feel something!" he cried. "Becky, I think you might be right!"

We all held our breath as slowly, carefully, he pulled a rolled up, yellow, crinkly piece of paper from the trumpet.

It was the lost Christmas song.

And this was the first time anyone was seeing it since Anna Kirkland hid it all those years ago. . . .

Love,
Becky

December 24

Wednesday

Dear God,

Happy happy Christmas Eve!

Do you know what? Yesterday was so exciting, I forgot to tear the link off my Christmas countdown chain!

So I will tear it off now, God.

And I will tear off the one for today, too.

● ● ●

This was one of the best days I ever had.

Bobby, my mother, and I had so much fun at the Church Family Christmas Eve Party!!!!

The best part of all was when we went

into the sanctuary and lit candles and sang Christmas carols.

Pastor and Mrs. Bennett sang Pastor Kirkland's Christmas song while Curtis, from my Sunday school class, strummed the guitar. It was *so beautiful*!!!! It was all about the angels singing to the shepherds about baby Jesus being born. I thought about how Anna must have listened to her father sing it, and that made me miss my own father. But I still felt Christmasy and peaceful.

Pastor Bennett explained to everyone why the song had been lost all those years. And when he explained how it had been found again, everyone turned and smiled at me. It was kind of embarrassing, but very, very nice!

Love,
Becky

December 25

Thursday

Dear God,

Merry, Merry, Merry, Merry, Merry CHRISTMAS!!!!!! Bobby, my mother, and I opened our presents early this morning.

I don't know why Bobby gave me a box of dog biscuits. Maybe they're for the dogs I walk. He also gave me a leash. I guess I can use that on my job, too, but Fifi and Patches already have their own leashes.

When I asked him about my presents, Bobby just laughed as if it was the funniest joke in the world. But I said thank you anyway. Just to be polite.

117

My mother gave me a manicure set and a skirt and sweater and a couple of new books.

LATER

Dear God,

We are back from Aunt Rosa's and as you know, she didn't give me a math game. She gave me dog dishes—one for water and one for food. I thought to myself, "What's going on?"

AND THEN!!!!!!!!!!!!!!!!

My mother brought out my *real* present from her and Bobby. I named him No-el, because I got him at Christmas.

Do you know what, God? It's very hard to write with a puppy jumping on your lap and licking your face!

Love,

Becky

If you enjoyed this book in The Kids from Apple Street Church series, you'll want to sneak a look at the diaries of all the kids in Miss Jenkins's Sunday school class.

1. Mary Jo Bennett
2. Danny Petrowski
3. Julie Chang
4. Pug McConnell
5. Becky Garcia
6. Curtis Anderson

You'll find these books at a Christian bookstore. Or write to Chariot Books, 850 N. Grove, Elgin, IL 60120.